Dinosaur Kisses

David Ezra Stein

WALKER BOOKS
AND SUBSIDIARIES
LONDON · BOSTON · SYDNEY · AUCKLAND

After being in an egg
for some time, Dinah hatched out.

There was so much to see and do.

She tried this ...

STOMP!

and that ...

CHOMP!

Then she saw a kiss.

She decided to try that next.

"I will kiss you!"

WHOMP!

"Whoops," said Dinah.

"I will kiss you!"

CHOMP!

"Whoops," said Dinah.

"I will kiss you!"

"This time, if I'm really, really
careful and I use only my lips ...

then I can do it!"

But she ate him.

"Whoops," said Dinah. "Not good."

Dinah went back to her egg to think.

Then she heard a noise.

KRAK!

"Hello," said the baby.

Dinah said, "I will kiss you!"

"What's kiss?" said the baby.

Dinah said, "Kiss is this!"

CHOMP!

The baby said, "Kiss is this?"

STOMP!

"Kiss!"

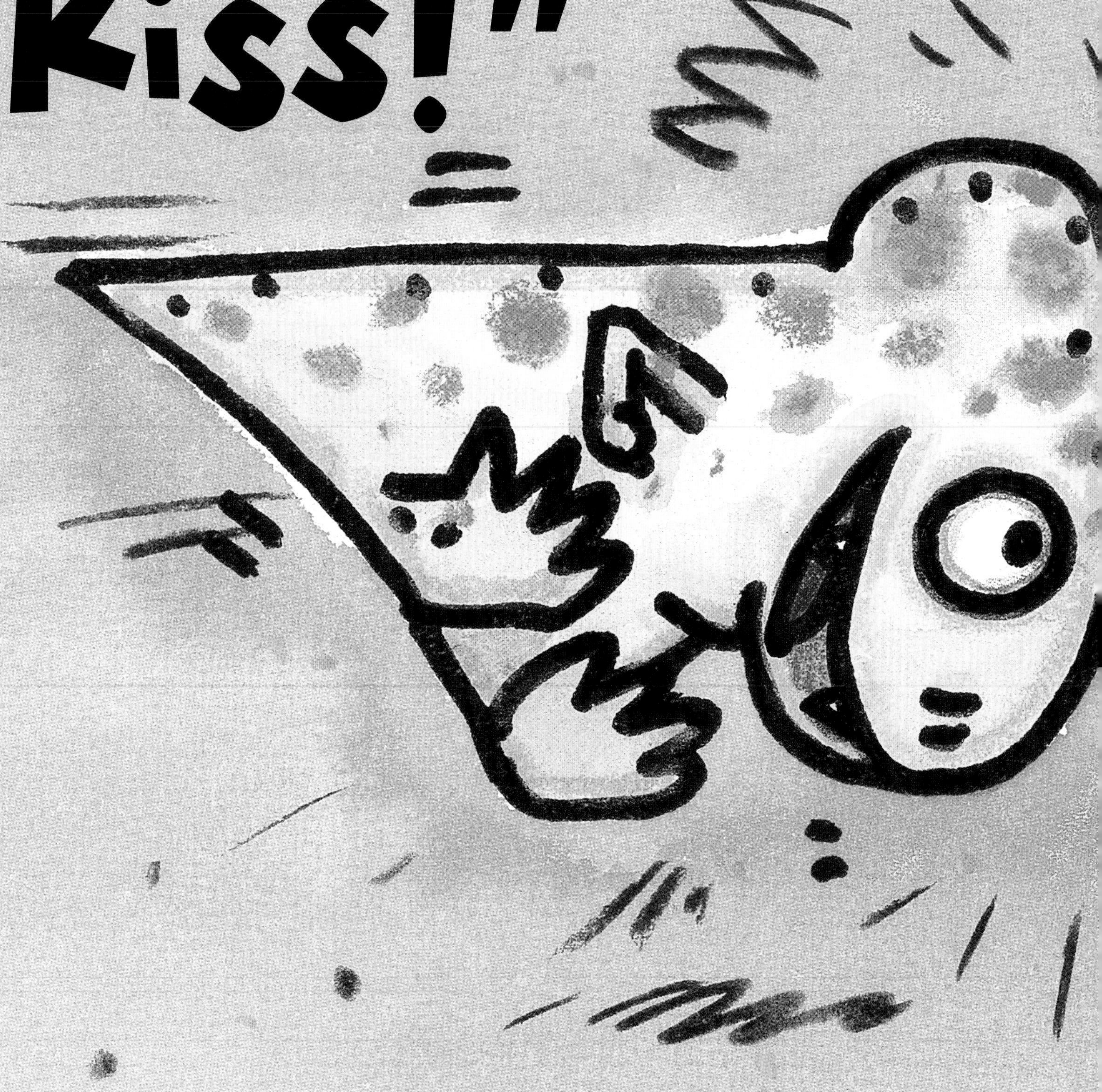

Ha! Ha! Ha!

To Ginger and to the Chompers, Stompers and Whompers of Kew Gardens

First published 2014 by Walker Books Ltd
87 Vauxhall Walk, London SE11 5HJ

This edition published 2015

2 4 6 8 10 9 7 5 3 1

© 2013 David Ezra Stein

The right of David Ezra Stein to be identified as author/illustrator of this work has been
asserted by him in accordance with the Copyright, Designs and Patents Act 1988

This book has been typeset in Stone Hinge

Printed in China

British Library Cataloguing in Publication Data:
a catalogue record for this book is available from the British Library

ISBN 978-1-4063-5946-6

www.walker.co.uk